PUFFIN BOOKS

BAD KITTY

VS
UNCLE MURRAY

Nick Bruel is the author and illustrator of the bestselling Bad Kitty series. He is also a freelance cartoonist and illustrator and lives with his wife and daughter in New York.

Books by Nick Bruel

BAD KITTY GETS A BATH
BAD KITTY HAPPY BIRTHDAY
BAD KITTY VS UNCLE MURRAY

BAD KITTY

VS UNCLE MURRAY

NICK BRUEL

PUFFIN

PUFFIN BOOKS

Published by the Penguin Group
Penguin Books Ltd, 80 Strand, London WC2R 0RL, England
Penguin Group (USA) Inc., 375 Hudson Street, New York, New York 10014, USA
Penguin Group (Canada), 90 Eglinton Avenue East, Suite 700, Toronto, Ontario, Canada M4P 2Y3
(a division of Pearson Penguin Canada Inc.)
Penguin Ireland, 25 St Stephen's Green, Dublin 2, Ireland (a division of Penguin Books Ltd)
Penguin Group (Australia), 250 Camberwell Road, Camberwell, Victoria 3124, Australia
(a division of Pearson Australia Group Pty Ltd)
Penguin Books India Pvt Ltd, 11 Community Centre, Panchsheel Park, New Delhi – 110 017, India
Penguin Group (NZ), 67 Apollo Drive, Rosedale, Auckland 0632, New Zealand
(a division of Pearson New Zealand Ltd)
Penguin Books (South Africa) (Pty) Ltd, 24 Sturdee Avenue, Rosebank, Johannesburg 2196, South Africa

Penguin Books Ltd, Registered Offices: 80 Strand, London WC2R 0RL, England

puffinbooks.com

First published in the USA by Roaring Brook Press 2010
Published in Great Britain in Puffin Books 2011
001 – 10 9 8 7 6 5 4 3 2 1

Copyright © Nick Bruel, 2010
All rights reserved

The moral right of the author/illustrator has been asserted

Printed in Great Britain by Clays Ltd, St Ives plc

British Library Cataloguing in Publication Data
A CIP catalogue record for this book is available from the British Library

ISBN: 978-0-141-33596-4

www.greenpenguin.co.uk

MIX
Paper from
responsible sources
FSC™ C018179

Penguin Books is committed to a sustainable
future for our business, our readers and our
planet. This book is made from paper certified
by the Forest Stewardship Council.

To Neal

• CONTENTS •

•CHAPTER ONE•

PUSSYCAT PARADISE

WELCOME, KITTY!

Welcome to Pussycat Paradise, where everything you see is made entirely out of **FOOD** – food for your belly!

The mountains are made out of chunks of dried cat food. The trees are made out of sausages and bacon. Cans of cat food grow out of the ground. And the grass is made out of catnip.

Yes, Kitty! Eat! EAT! Food is everywhere! The rocks are made out of turkey and giblets. The soil is made out of tuna fish. Even the rivers flow with beef gravy.

And the best part, of course, is that YOU are the only one here! No dogs to hound you. No people to make you take a bath. There is no one else here. Only you.

Be careful, Kitty. Don't touch that can. It's the only thing holding up that gigantic chicken liver.

OH NO! TOO LATE! The gigantic chicken liver is going to fall! Look out, Kitty! LOOK OUT!!

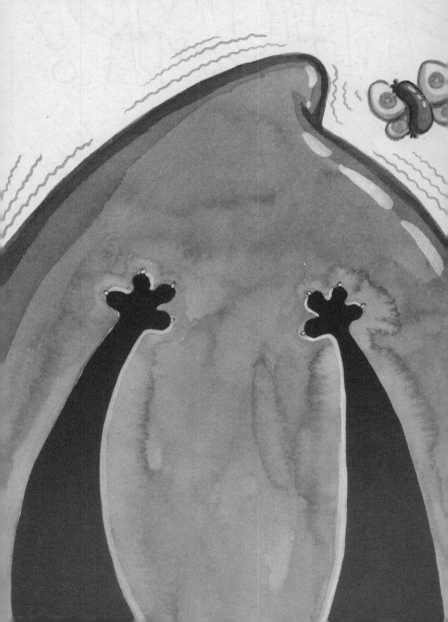

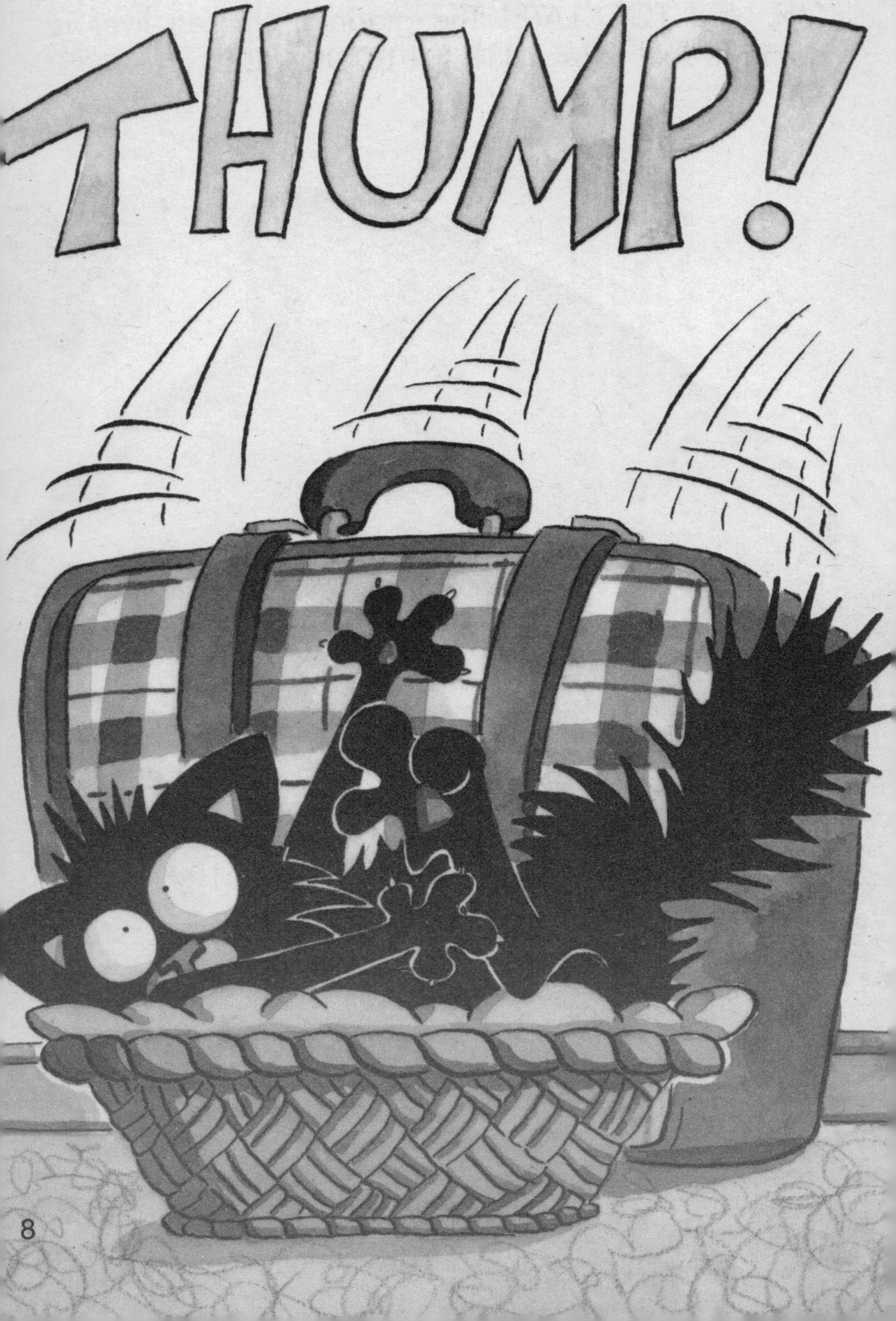
THUMP!

WHOOPS!

Sorry, Kitty. I hope I didn't wake you when I dropped the suitcase.

That's right, Kitty. We're going on a little trip. We'll be gone for a while.

Sorry, Kitty. You're not going with us. You'll have to stay at home with Puppy.

Oh, don't be like that, Kitty. We'll be back in just a week. And when we get back, we'll have a REALLY BIG SURPRISE for you!

That's right, Kitty. **A REALLY BIG SURPRISE!** You like surprises, don't you?

In the meantime, Kitty, you won't be alone. We've found someone who's going to stay here and feed you and take good care of you and Puppy while we're away.

In fact, that must be him!

Where did Kitty go? Oh, well. At least Puppy is excited to see who's here.

IT'S GOOD OL' UNCLE MURRAY!

There you are, Kitty. Don't you want to say "Hi" to good ol' Uncle Murray?

Awww! You're a good dog, aren't you?

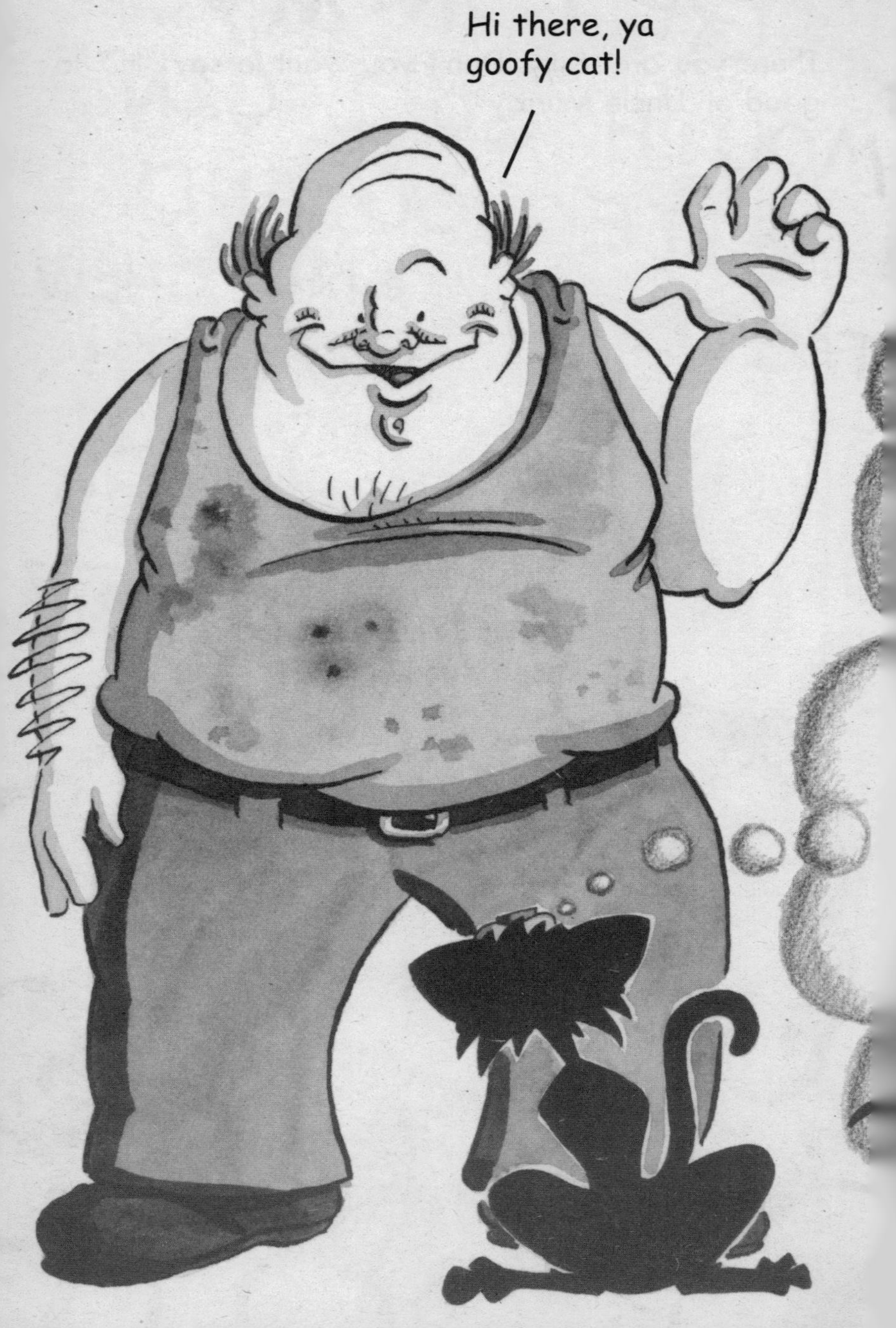
Hi there, ya goofy cat!

GET IN MY MOUTH SO I CAN BITE YOU AND TASTE YOU AND CHEW YOU WITH MY BIG, SHARP TEETH!

22

UNCLE MURRAY'S FUN FACTS

I was just wondering about that.

WHY ARE SOME CATS AFRAID OF PEOPLE?

No one ever talks about a "scaredy-giraffe" or a "scaredy-penguin" or even a "scaredy-dog", but everyone's heard of "scaredy-cats"! That's because cats use fear as a very valuable tool for survival.

The average weight of a cat is only around 4.5 kilos. Imagine what your life would be like if you lived with someone who was almost TWENTY TIMES BIGGER than you! That's what life is like for a cat living with a human being. Having good reflexes to avoid being stepped on or sat upon is very important.

CAT: AROUND 4.5 KILOS.

BIG, FAT, GOOFY-LOOKING AUTHOR OF THIS BOOK: 84 KILOS.

REALLY? DOES THIS BOOK MAKE ME LOOK FAT?

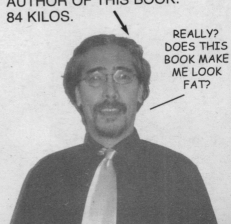

But sometimes a cat's fear of people can become exaggerated. Sometimes this happens when a kitten is raised without any human contact. It can also happen if a cat or a kitten has had a bad experience with a person.

But I'm a nice guy! I wouldn't hurt a fly, much less a dog or a cat, no matter how goofy it is.

It doesn't matter. A cat's instinct always tells her to be careful around people, especially strangers. The best way to get a cat to grow used to you is to be patient, be gentle, be quiet and try not to take the cat's reaction to you too personally.

And one more thing . . . Try not to make any sudden, loud noises. Cats hate that.

No loud, sudden noises. Got it! What kind of jerk do you think I am? Everybody knows that!

27

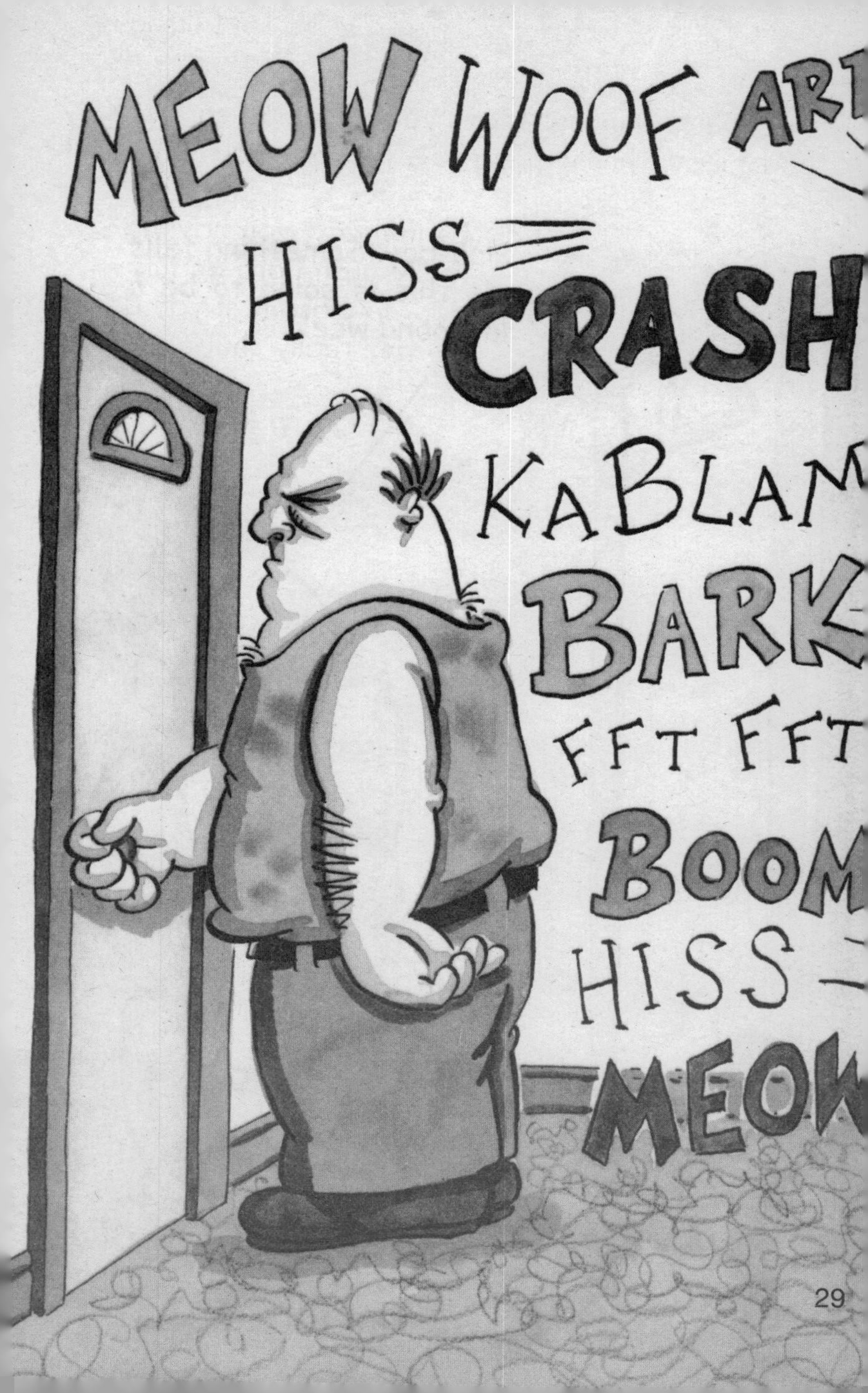
MEOW
WOOF
AR
HISS
CRASH
KaBLAM
BARK
FFT FFT
BOOM
HISS
MEOW

•CHAPTER TWO•
HIDE!

You know what, dog . . . I think the best thing to do right now is to sit down, relax, have some lunch and maybe watch a little . . .

35

I see you there pretending to be a dishcloth again, ya goofy cat! Don't scream at me. Don't scream at me. Don't scream at me. Don't scream at me. Don't scream at me. Don't scream at me . . .

39

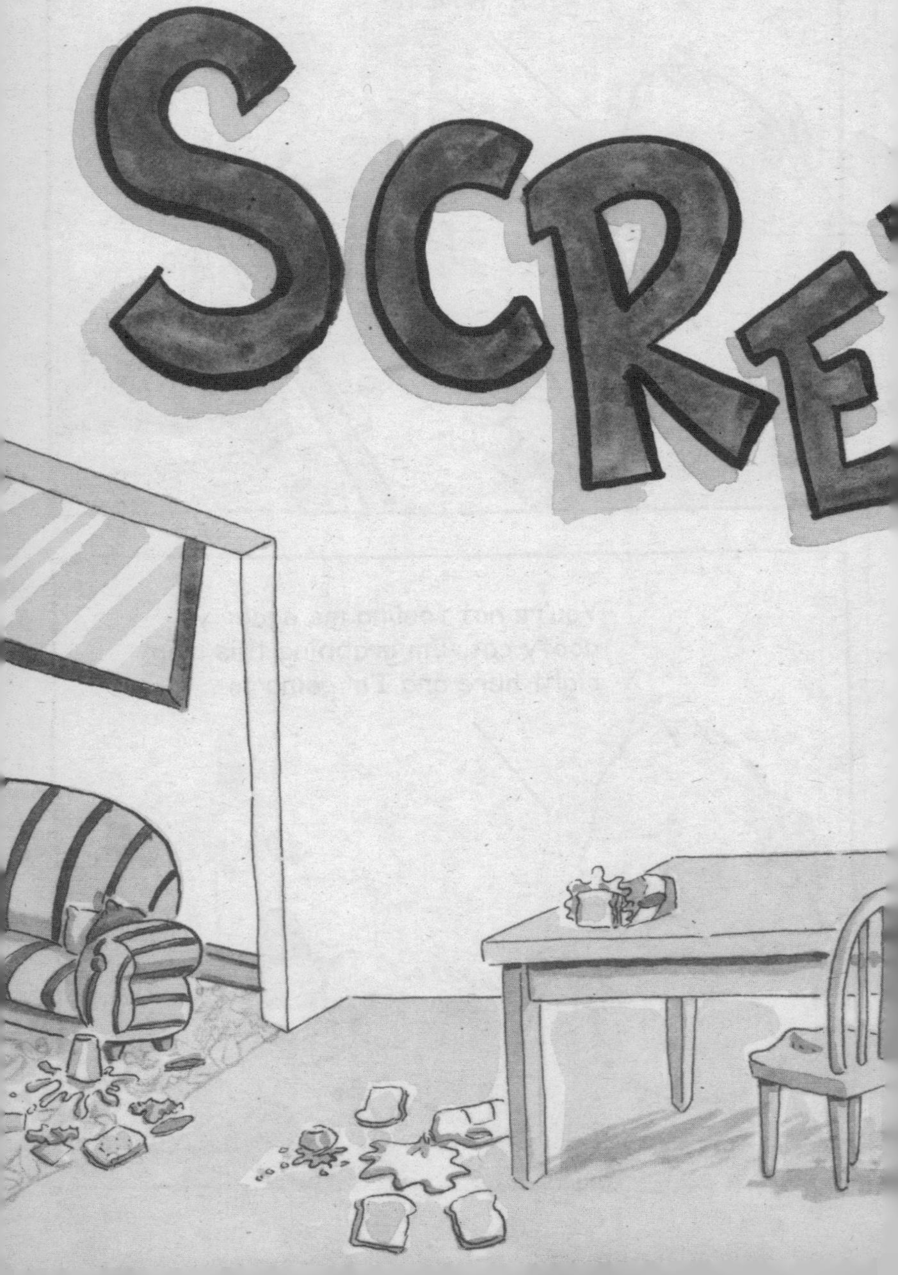
SCRE

All I really wanted was to
sit down, relax, have some
lunch and maybe watch a
little TV.

All I really wanted was to
sit down, relax, have some
lunch and maybe watch a
little TV.

All I really wanted was to
sit down, relax, have some
lunch and maybe watch a
little TV.

All I really wanted was to
sit down, relax, have some
lunch and maybe watch a
little TV.

•CHAPTER THREE•
THE KITTY DIARIES

TWO MINUTES LATER . . .
NO FOOD. NO WATER. MONSTER IS STILL OUT THERE. IT HAS BIG FEET. DOG SMELLS BAD.

EIGHTEEN MINUTES . . .

SO VERY, VERY, VERY HUNGRY! SMELLY, UGLY, STUPID DOG IS GONE. MONSTER MUST HAVE EATEN HIM. GOOD. BUT WHAT IS THIS?! NOW I SEE A ~~DELISHEEUS~~ ~~DEELICHUS~~ TASTY TURKEY LEG. COULD THIS BE TRUE?

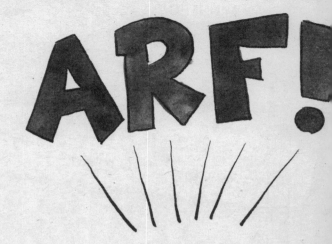

53

CHAPTER FOUR

UNCLE MURRAY STRIKES BACK

Y'know, . . . this stuff doesn't look half bad.

GOBBLE CHEW
MUNCH MASTICATE
GNAW SLURP
GULP
CHEW
YUM
KITTY
MUNCH
EAT
GOBBLE
GNAW

61

64

Y'know, dog . . . when I was just a kid, I had a pooch a lot like you. He was a good dog, too.

I named him Sam, and I found him lost and hungry in an alley near where I lived. He was all white except for some black spots on his face and one of his back legs.

Anyway, I still had half a sandwich on me from lunch so I tossed it to him. Boy, oh, boy was he happy to get some food into his little dog belly. You'd think he hadn't eaten anything in a year. It was just ham, after all. No mustard, even.

I used my belt as a lead and put it around Sam's neck. At first I thought he'd go crazy when I started to pull him, but he didn't. In fact, he barked and licked my hand the whole way home.

But there was a problem. My mother wouldn't let me keep Sam in the house 'cause my baby sister was real allergic to dogs. I guess it was true, 'cause she still is. I told my mom I would keep Sam only in my room, but she told me that wouldn't really work. She was right.

So I did the only thing I could think of . . . I took little Sam to a dog shelter where they'd feed him and take good care of him.

They were real nice to Sam there. He had his own little cage, and there were lots of other dogs there for him to talk to. But the best part was that they said I could come and visit him every day after school. So I did!

I went to visit Sam every single day, and each time he saw me he'd jump up and lick my face and wrestle me to the ground like he was sayin', "Gee, I'm really happy to see you! Where've you been?"

Each day, I taught him a new trick. I taught him to sit and to stay. I taught him to beg and to roll over. I even taught him geography. NAHHH! I'm just kidding about that last one. But he really was smart.

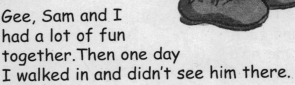

K-CHOO!

Gee, Sam and I had a lot of fun together. Then one day I walked in and didn't see him there.

A lady who worked at the shelter told me a family had come in just after I left the day before, fell in love with Sam, and took him home. She said they were real nice people and promised to feed him and take good care of him. But that didn't help. I started crying like Niagara Falls. He may not have lived with me, but Sam was <u>MY</u> <u>DOG</u>!

I thought for sure that I'd never see little Sam again.

But then, one day, about a year later, as I was walking through the park, I looked over and saw a little girl playing with a dog that looked a whole lot like my Sam. He was all white except for some black spots on his face and one of his back legs. It <u>was</u> him! And they were having a swell time. Sam was even doing some of the same tricks that <u>I</u> taught him.

It hurt me so much inside to see this little girl playing with my dog. <u>MY</u> <u>DOG</u>. But then I looked at how much fun they were having and how happy he looked, and I thought to myself . . . all I ever really wanted for that lost, hungry dog sitting alone in that alley was for someone to take him home and feed him and take good care of him. Right? And that's what I got.

I loved that dog, and now I knew that someone else loved that dog as much as me.

It was one of those days that was both real good and real bad at the same time.

71

WHY ARE CATS AFRAID OF VACUUM CLEANERS?

It's not the vacuum cleaner that frightens cats so much as the sudden, loud noise it makes. Most cats will react quickly to any sudden, loud noise like a car horn, or a firework, or someone yelling.

Cats can hear very, very well – even better than dogs. In fact, a cat can hear three times better than a human being. That's why a cat can hear a mouse rustling through the grass from 9 metres away. But it's also why loud noises are particularly painful for cats. And that's what inspires their fear.

RUSTLE

ZZZZZ... DING!

Fear of loud noises is another survival tool for cats. If a little noise is a signal that something to eat might be nearby, then a very loud noise is the same as a fire alarm held up next to their ears. And that means DANGER. And that means FIGHT or RUN AWAY.

When a cat is frightened, running away or hiding is a common response. But sometimes if a cat feels trapped or cornered, she'll stand still while unusual things happen to her body.

First, all the fur on her body will stand on end. Then the cat will arch her back up using all sixty of her vertebrae – humans have only thirty-four, by the way. This will make the cat look much bigger; a tactic it uses to intimidate its enemies. But the sign to be very aware of is when a cat has turned its ears back. A cat will do this when it feels like fighting back and wants to protect those sensitive ears. That is a clear sign to back away from a VERY angry cat that could attack you.

DANGER

MORE DANGER

LOTS AND LOTS OF DANGER

Never mind all that ear stuff! I gotta go grab that cat!

Here,
Kitty,
Kitty,
Kitty!

•CHAPTER FIVE•
CATCH THAT KITTY

*Hark!

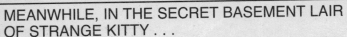
MEANWHILE, IN THE SECRET BASEMENT LAIR OF STRANGE KITTY . . .

DO YOU HEAR THAT, OLD CHUM? I DO BELIEVE I HEAR PLAINTIVE CRIES FOR HELP FROM OUR OLD FELINE FRIEND WITH THE BLACK FUR AND REBELLIOUS ATTITUDE!

HOLY CATNIP, S.K.! WE CAN'T IGNORE A PLAINTIVE CRY FOR HELP!

RIGHT YOU ARE, OLD BEAN! ONCE AGAIN, THE WORLD IS IN NEED OF . . .

CHAPTER SIX

KITTIES TO
THE RESCUE

I got you *HUFF*
trapped now, *PUFF*
ya goofy *HUFF* cat!

93

*Let us in, and I mean RIGHT MEOW!

Boy-oh-boy-oh-boy! This day just can't get any weirder.

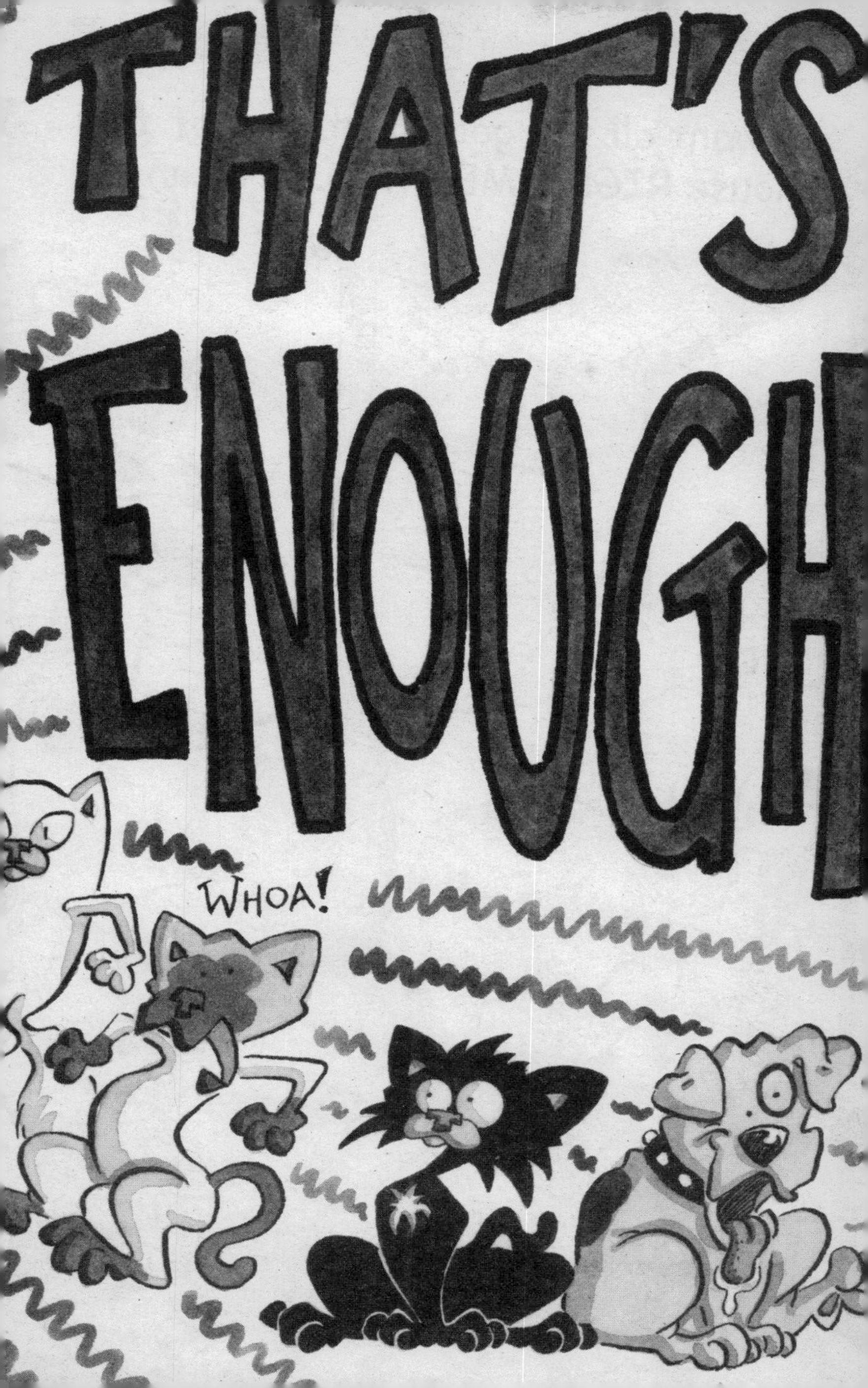
THAT'S ENOUGH
WHOA!

RIGHT
NOW!!

*Get ME OUT of here!

113

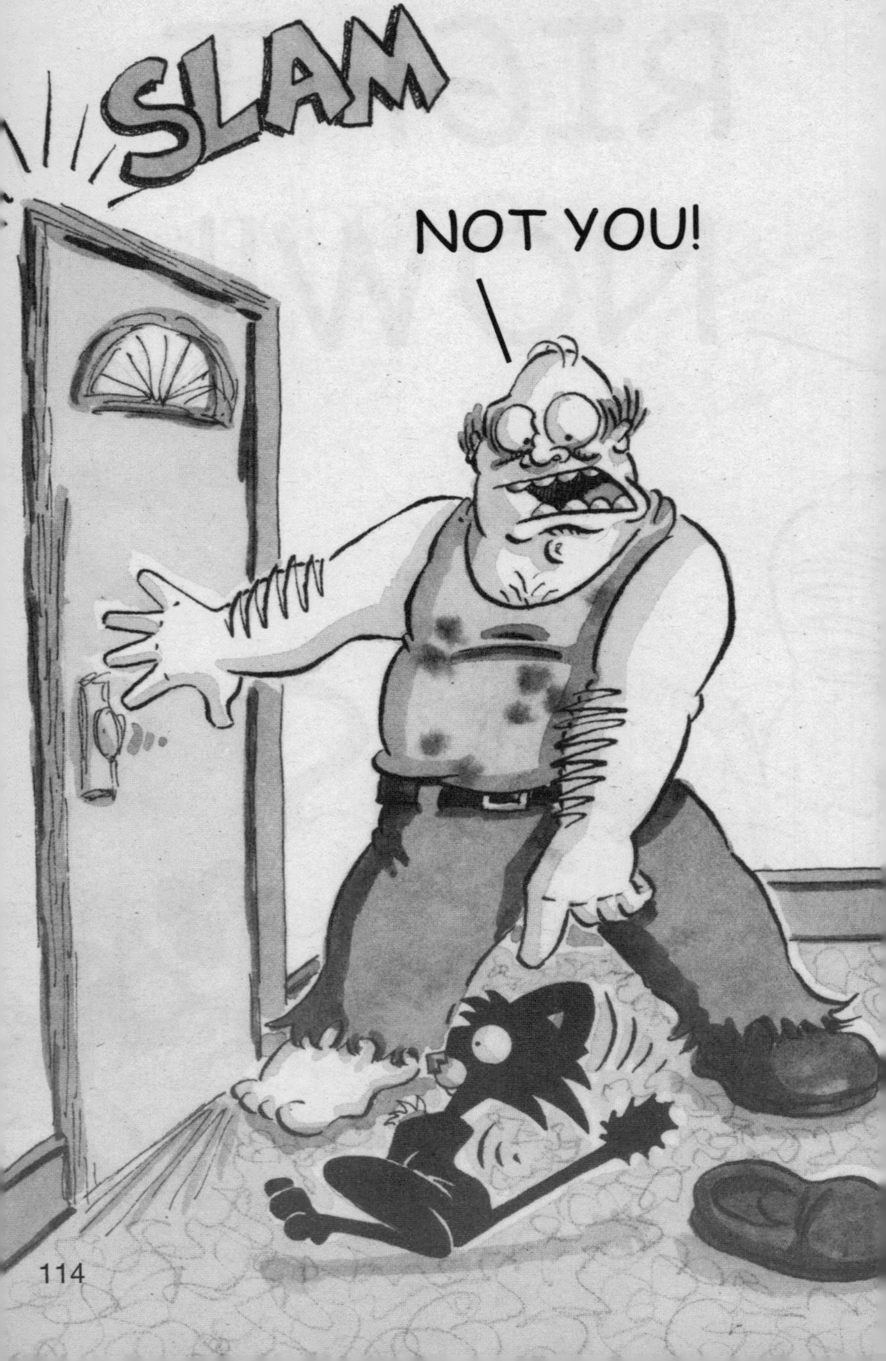
SLAM
NOT YOU!

That's right! You heard me! As soon as I open this door, I'll be free. FREE! No more goofy cats screaming in my face and eating my shoes. No more biting and scratching and chasing me down the street. Outside this door is a big, wonderful world where goofy cats don't turn into furry whirlwinds that hit me on the head with a spatula. And soon I will be a part of that world once again!

YAWN

120

121

•CHAPTER SEVEN•
KITTY ON HER OWN

MEOW?

WHY ARE SOME CATS AFRAID OF BEING ALONE?

Cats are independent animals. There's no question about that. They're very good at taking care of themselves in the wild. But when cats have become house cats, they usually become "bonded" with their owner.

When a cat becomes very close, even dependent on a human being for food or protection, that's called "bonding".

And sometimes when that bond is broken, even for just a little while, some cats might exhibit "separation anxiety". Have you ever seen a baby begin to cry just because her Mommy has left the room for just a few seconds? That's a good example of "separation anxiety" and even cats can get it.

Leave cats alone for too long and they'll start to cry out to see if anyone is in the house, just like a baby. Sometimes they'll lose their appetite and not eat.

The most anxious cats will even pull out clumps of their own fur because of nervousness.

The solution for all fears is to let the cat gradually grow used to whatever scares them. Cats can adapt very quickly.

If a cat is afraid of people, keep your distance and step a little closer day by day, while also letting her come to you under her own power. If your cat is afraid of loud noises, try to keep the sound down at first if possible, and then increase the exposure a little bit each day.

And if the cat is afraid of being alone, give her time to adjust as she learns that you'll eventually return. She'll hate being alone at first, but in time she'll learn that there's nothing to be afraid of once you keep coming back.

131

I made a promise to feed you all week and take good care of you all week. And I'm going to keep that promise even if you act mean and goofy to me all week.

137

Although . . . something tells me this is STILL going to be a very long week.

• EPILOGUE •

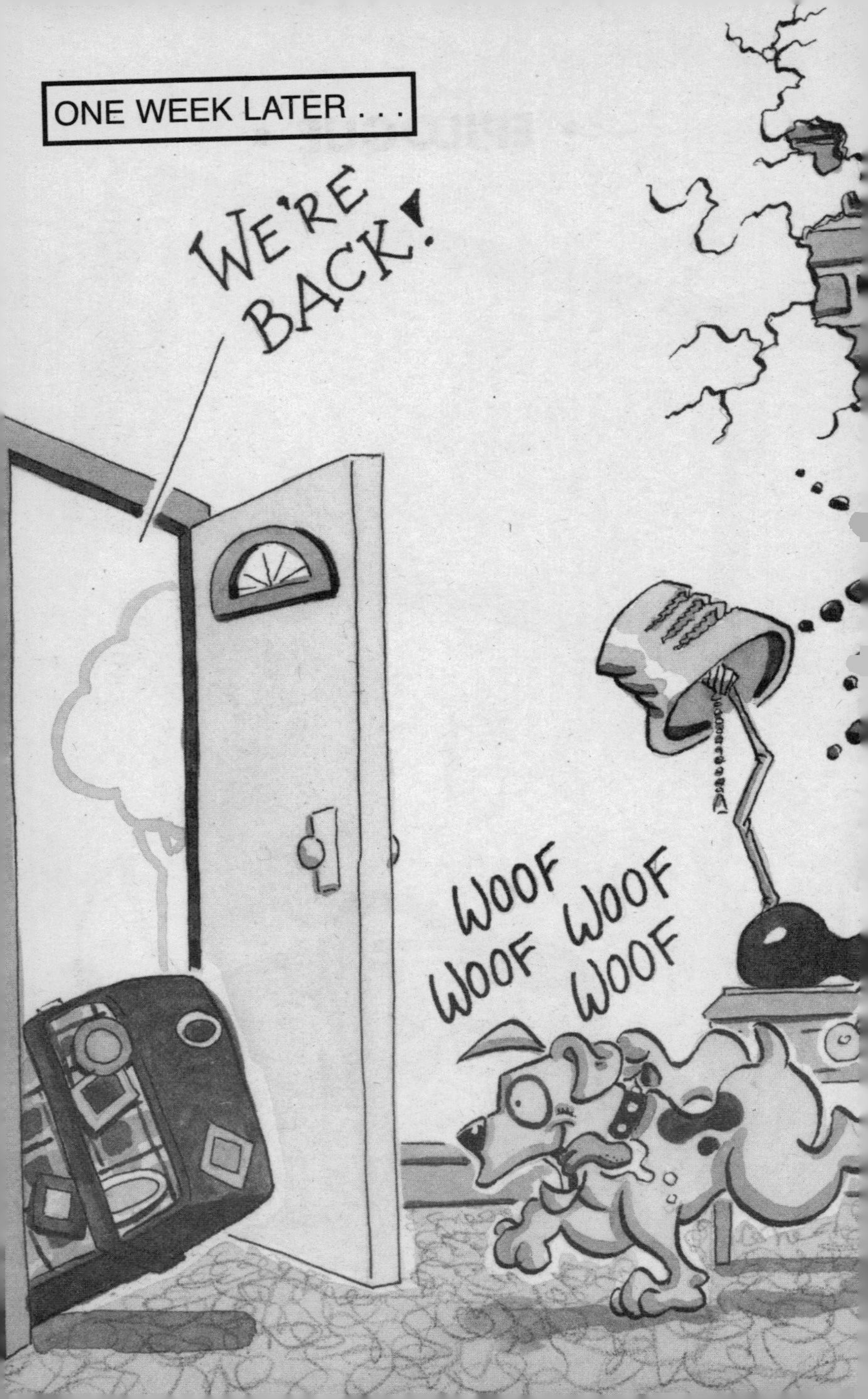
ONE WEEK LATER . . .
WE'RE BACK!
WOOF WOOF WOOF WOOF WOOF

Thank you so much, Uncle Murray, for taking such good care of Kitty and Puppy. I know they can be a real handful. I hope they weren't too much trouble.

Fish.

What did you say, Uncle Murray?

Fish don't bite or scream or chase you around the house or hit you on the head with a spatula. All they do is swim around and make nice little bubbles that don't hurt anybody. And they're pretty. Pretty like little rainbows. Fish.

Fish don't bite or scream or chase you around the house or . . .

143

Hmmm . . . Oh, well. Goodbye, Uncle Murray. And thanks again.

HI, KITTY!
Did you miss us?

HMPF

Awwww! We missed you, too, Kitty!

HEY! Do you remember that REALLY BIG SURPRISE we promised you? Do you? DO YOU?!

Well, here she is!

To be continued . . .

• APPENDIX •
A SELECTION OF PHOBIAS

A "phobia" is a strong fear of a specific object or a specific situation. Most of the time the fear is irrational, meaning that the person who has the phobia really has nothing to fear. For instance, a boy might be afraid of worms (Scoleciphobia), but that doesn't mean the boy has any real reason to be afraid of worms, other than he thinks they're scary and doesn't want them anywhere near him.

Sixteen per cent of the people who live in the United Kingdom have a phobia. That's around ten million people! This means that phobias are very common and nothing to be ashamed of.

We've seen a lot of different examples of fear in this book. The following is a small selection of over five hundred known phobias.

Agrizoophobia – Fear of wild animals.

Ailurophobia (also, Elurophobia) – Fear of cats.

Amychophobia – Fear of scratches or being scratched.

Cynophobia – Fear of dogs.

Ligyrophobia (also, Phonophobia) – Fear of loud noises, also, fear of voices or one's own voice.

Lilapsophobia – Fear of hurricanes or tornadoes.

Monophobia (also Autophobia) – Fear of being alone.

Olfactophobia (also, Osmophobia) – Fear of smells or odors.

Peladophobia – Fear of bald people.

Phagophobia – Fear of swallowing, eating, or being eaten.

Pnigophobia – Fear of being choked or smothered.

Teratophobia – Fear of monsters.